WESTERN ISLES LIBRARIES

Readers are requested to take great care of the item while in
their possession, and to point out ~~~~~~~~~~ ey may
notice in them to th~

This item should be ~~~~~~~~~~~~~~~~~~~~~ t date
stamped below, but ~~~~~~~~~~~~~~~~~~~ may
be granted when des~~~~~~~~~~~~~~~~~~ NTRE

Date of return	Date of return	Date of return
BOX 32	PI-3 BOX4	
PI-3 Box 4	" "	
" "		
Bernera Box 4 Dec 20		
PI-3 Box 4		
" "		

Written by Richard Dungworth

Illustrated by Sarah Horne

A catalogue record for this book is available from the British Library

Published by Ladybird Books Ltd.
A Penguin Company
Penguin Books Ltd., 80 Strand, London, WC2R 0RL
Penguin Books Australia Ltd., Camberwell, Victoria, Australia
Penguin Group (NZ) 67 Apollo Drive, Rosedale,
North Shore 0632, New Zealand

001 – 10 9 8 7 6 5 4 3 2 1
© LADYBIRD BOOKS LTD MMXII

LADYBIRD and the device of a Ladybird are trademarks of Ladybird Books Ltd

ISBN: 978-1-40931-241-3

Printed in Great Britain by Clays Ltd, St Ives plc

Mixed Sources
Product group from well-managed
forests and other controlled sources
www.fsc.org   Cert no. SA-COC-001592
© 1996 Forest Stewardship Council

FSC

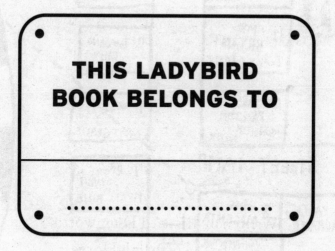

THIS LADYBIRD
BOOK BELONGS TO

....

Tom and Daisy live on Genie Street, with their mum and dad.

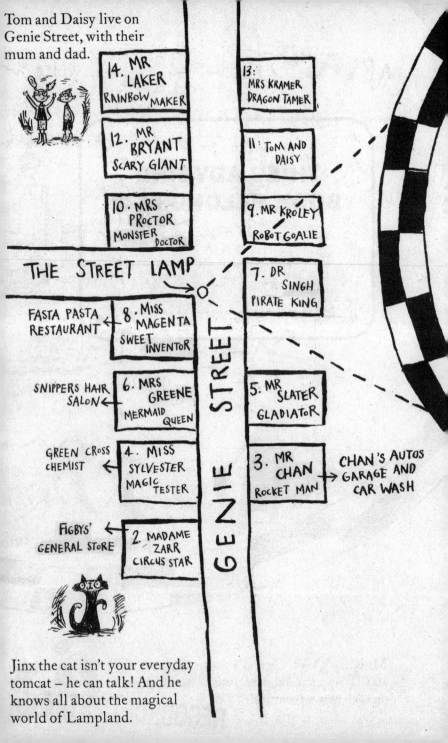

14. MR LAKER
RAINBOW MAKER

13: MRS KRAMER DRAGON TAMER

12. MR BRYANT
SCARY GIANT

11: TOM AND DAISY

10. MRS PROCTOR
MONSTER DOCTOR

9. MR KROLEY
ROBOT GOALIE

THE STREET LAMP

7. DR SINGH
PIRATE KING

FASTA PASTA RESTAURANT ←

8. MISS MAGENTA
SWEET INVENTOR

SNIPPERS HAIR SALON ←

6. MRS GREENE
MERMAID QUEEN

5. MR SLATER
GLADIATOR

GREEN CROSS CHEMIST ←

4. MISS SYLVESTER
MAGIC TESTER

3. MR CHAN
ROCKET MAN

→ CHAN'S AUTOS GARAGE AND CAR WASH

FIGBYS' GENERAL STORE ←

2. MADAME ZARR
CIRCUS STAR

GENIE STREET

Jinx the cat isn't your everyday tomcat – he can talk! And he knows all about the magical world of Lampland.

LAMPLAND

to the Noom

Wild Isles

Launch pad

the Seventh Sea

Sweet Factory

Rainbow Meadows

Techno Town

City of Ancients

Castle Kinghold

to Crossbone Island

Mermaid Reef

Red Dragon Hills

Fairy Forest

Land of the Giants

Monster Mountains

Mr Mistry, Genie Street's postman, gives Tom and Daisy a special parcel which sends them on each new adventure!

Mrs Greene

MERMAID QUEEN

Contents

Chapter One
A Visit to Snippers

'Ready?' Tom asked Daisy.

'Ready!' replied his sister.

Tom put a hand on the magic street lamp. He began to rub the lamp post carefully.

'*Once up… once down…*' he chanted. He knew that only the right kind of rub would do the trick. '*Then three times round and round…*'

The magic street lamp lit up.
It cast a bright purple glow.

'It's working!' cried Daisy.
She was very excited. She
knew that this was the first
step into a world of adventure.
The street lamp's purple light
had led her and Tom to this
other world before. It was
called Lampland. It was a
marvellous, magical place.

A ball of purple light shot
from the top of the street lamp.

'Watch where it g–'

But, even before Tom could
finish, the ball of light had
found its target. It had hit
the doorway of Snippers,
the hairdresser's salon.

Tom and Daisy hurried
to take a look.

There was a purple glow
around the edges of the
shop's door.

'Shall we?' said Daisy.

'Allow me!' grinned Tom.

He was reaching for the door handle, when –

POP-POP-POP-POP-POP!

Something was racing along the road towards them. It was making a very peculiar noise and a big cloud of pale yellow smoke.

The mystery vehicle pulled up at the kerb. The noise stopped. The smoke slowly cleared.

Chapter Two
Deep Trouble

It was a go-kart. The driver was a small, plump man in a smart purple uniform.

'Mr Mistry!' cried Daisy.

'Hullo! Hullo!' beamed the Genie Street postman. 'Now that's the way to travel!' He patted the steering wheel. 'Runs on lemonade, you know! Now to business!'

He reached under his seat, pulled out a parcel and handed it to Daisy. She read its label.

'It's for Mrs Greene,' she said.

Mrs Greene cut Daisy's hair. Daisy liked her.

Daisy was about to ask Mr Mistry what the 'HM' in front of Mrs Greene's name stood for, when –

POP-POP-POP-POP-POP!

The go-kart, and Mr Mistry, disappeared in another cloud of lemony smoke.

'Come on! Let's find Mrs Greene!' said Tom. He pulled open the door to Snippers – and stared.

'But how…?' murmured Daisy.

The shop floor wasn't there any more. Instead there was a large pool of water.

Without warning the door swung shut. It nudged the children forward. They cried out, then – SPLASH! They plunged into the pool.

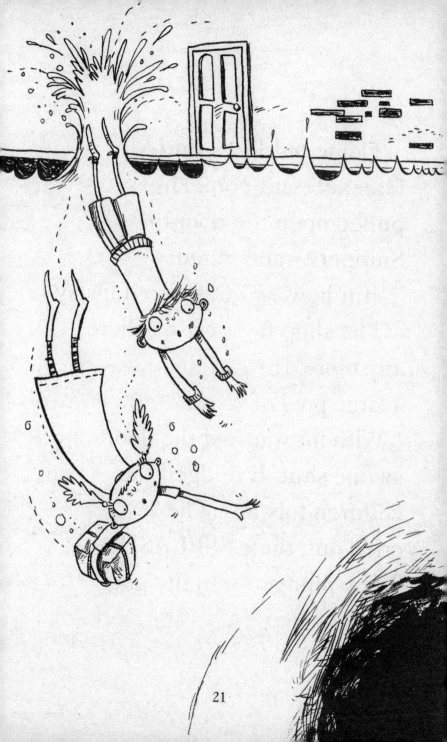

Chapter Three
The Mermaid Queen

The next few seconds were a blur for Tom. He sank deeper and deeper underwater. He did his best to get back to the surface, but it was no good.

Panic rose inside him. He was desperate to breathe.

Then suddenly long webbed fingers grasped him from behind.

The hands spun Tom round. He found himself looking into the green eyes of a stranger – a stranger who was half man, half fish.

The merman pursed his lips. A silvery bubble began to swell from them. When it had grown to the size of a beachball, the merman grasped it in both hands. He pushed it down over Tom's head.

Tom immediately found that he could breathe.

Daisy was bobbing in the sea, not far away. A second merman had given her a breathing bubble just like Tom's. She was pointing.

'Tom, look! Look who it is!'

A beautiful carriage floated nearby. It was made of shells, and pulled by a giant seahorse. Another merman, with a spiky trident, held the reins.

And sitting in the carriage, wearing a golden crown, was Mrs Greene.

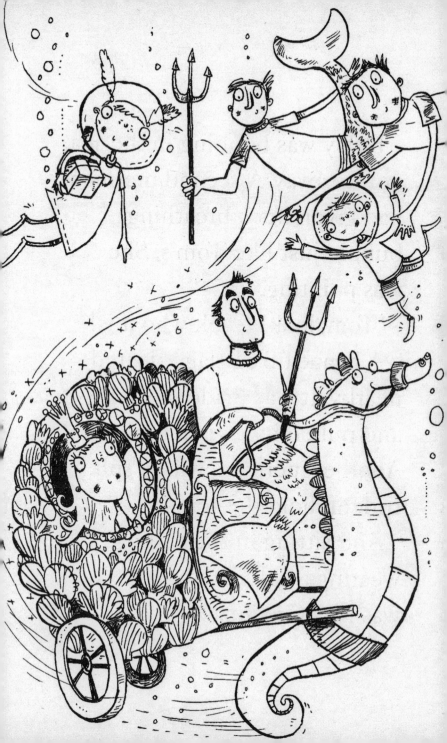

Chapter Four
The Pearl Fields

Mrs Greene, Mermaid Queen, beckoned urgently to the children. 'Quickly! In you get! These are dangerous waters!'

Tom and Daisy did as they were told. They swam over to the royal carriage and climbed in. The merman driver flicked his reins.

The seahorse-drawn carriage sped over a beautiful reef. Everywhere Tom and Daisy looked, there were strange underwater plants, dazzling fish and *lots* of oyster shells.

The queen reached out to grab one. She showed them the enormous pearl inside.

'These are the Pearl Fields,' she told them. 'My people depend on them. We harvest the pearls to trade with the rest of Lampland.'

The queen's face saddened.

'But it is no longer safe to harvest our pearls,' she said. 'I have ridden out with my guards today to see for myself how they lie uncollected. A great danger has come to the Pearl Fields!'

'What "great danger"?' asked Tom. Daisy nudged him. 'Your Majesty,' Tom added quickly.

Before the queen could answer, there was a loud, blood-curdling howl.

Chapter Five
Mercats and Hairbrushes

'MeeOOOWWWW! *You're treading on my paw!*' howled a familiar voice.

'Jinx!' cried Tom and Daisy.

Their old friend from Genie Street appeared from under the carriage seat. He looked rather cross – and *very* different from the last time they had seen him!

'It's rude to stare,' Jinx reminded them grumpily. 'To be honest, being a mercat – even a royal one – isn't my thing. Cat and fish don't mix. I keep wanting to eat my own fish tail. It's very tiresome!'

He looked at Daisy.

'Don't you have something for Her Majesty?' he purred.

'Oh! Of course!' said Daisy. She was still clutching the Special Delivery parcel.

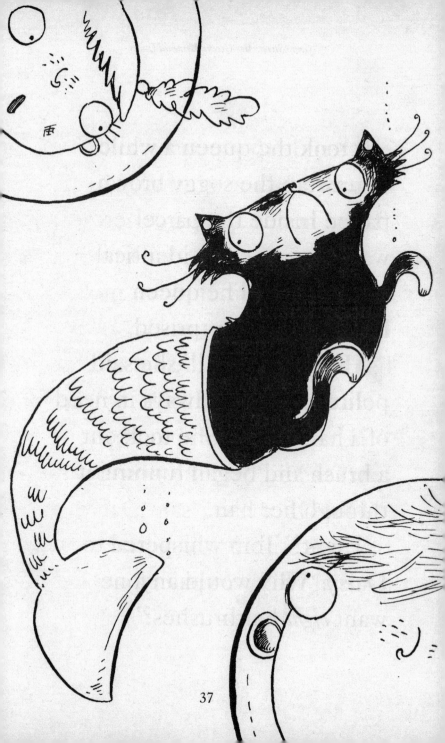

It took the queen a while to unwrap the soggy brown paper. Inside the parcel was a box of eight identical hairbrushes. The queen looked a little surprised.

'How delightful!' she said politely. 'One is always in need of a hairbrush!' She took out a brush and began running it through her hair.

'Eight?' Tom whispered to Daisy. 'Why would anyone want *eight* hairbrushes?'

The queen continued to groom her long blonde hair. 'It does get in such *awful* knots, you know!' she said. 'I've tried having attendants to brush it, but they just end up pulling it!'

Tom wasn't really listening any more. He was gazing ahead, wide-eyed.

'Now that,' he said, 'is *awesome*!'

The merpeople's underwater city had just come into view.

Chapter Six
Shipwreck!

Even from a distance, Reef City looked stunning. Its shining walls and towers were decorated with thousands of brightly coloured shells.

The city was still a little way off when Tom spotted something else.

'Look, Daisy! There's a wreck! A *real* shipwreck!'

The children begged the queen to stop the carriage so they could explore the shipwreck.

'Very well!' agreed the queen at last. 'But only for a few moments. I want us all safely back in my palace as soon as possible!'

Tom and Daisy swam down to the wreck. It was everything they had hoped for.

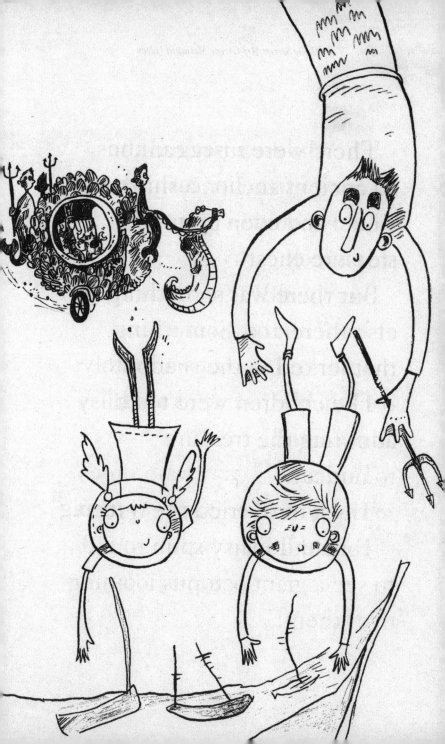

There were rusty cannons, an ancient anchor, a ship's wheel and even a sunken treasure chest.

But there was something else there, too. Something that lurked in the shadows.

The children were too busy admiring the treasure to notice…

'Look out!' cried the queen.

Tom and Daisy spun round to see a giant octopus looming over them!

'I guess we know what the "great danger" is now!' squeaked Tom.

In his hurry to get away, Tom bumped into the open lid of the treasure chest. It slammed shut.

'Tom! Help!' shrieked Daisy. 'My hair is trapped!'

Tom tried desperately to lift the chest's heavy lid. But it wouldn't budge.

The octopus was nearly upon them now. It really was *huge*.

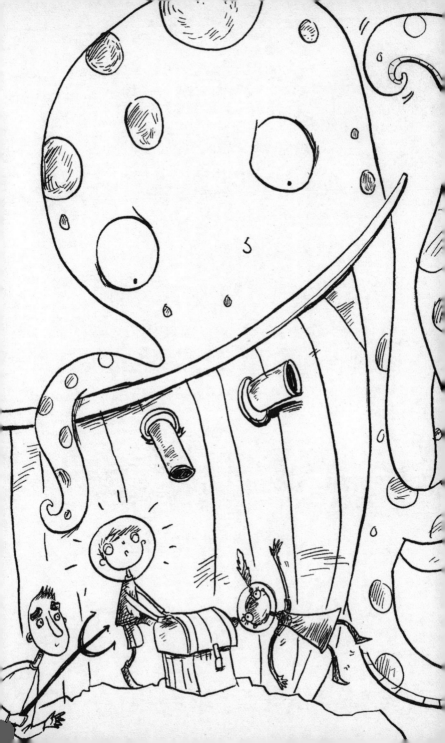

Chapter Seven
Daisy's Great Idea

The octopus reached out for
Daisy with one of its thick,
snaking tentacles.

The tentacle reached past
her and carefully lifted the
lid of the treasure chest.
Daisy's hair came free.

Daisy stared at the huge sea
creature. 'Thank you!' she said
in a tiny voice.

The octopus reached out with another of its tentacles. This time it *did* touch Daisy, but only to stroke her hair.

The merman guard suddenly came rushing through the water with his spiky trident at the ready.

'No! Stop!' cried Daisy. 'Can't you see? He's friendly!'

The guard lowered his weapon. He looked very surprised as the octopus began to stroke *his* hair, too.

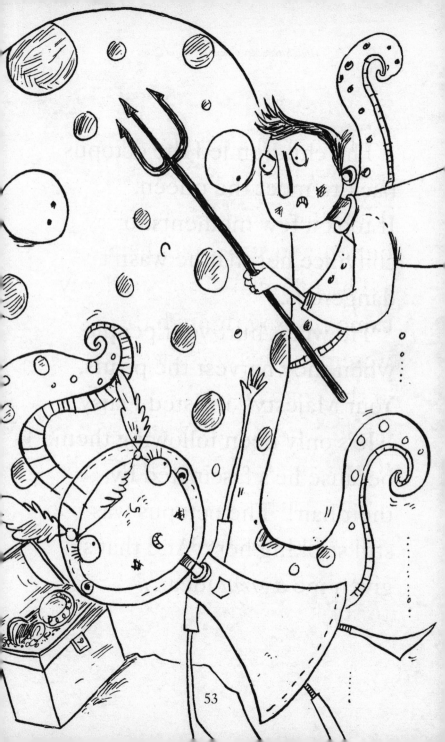

The children led the octopus
back to meet the queen.
It took a few moments to
convince her that he wasn't
dangerous.

'He won't hurt your people
when they harvest the pearls,
Your Majesty!' insisted Daisy.
'He's only been following them
because he's fascinated by
their hair!' The octopus was
still stroking hers. 'And that's
given me a *great* idea...'

Chapter Eight
The Queen's New Attendant

Daisy and Tom were floating in the throne room of the Mermaid Queen's palace, at the heart of Reef City.

The queen sat on her throne of shiny pink shells. Jinx was on her lap.

And the octopus was there, too, brushing the queen's hair – with *eight* hairbrushes.

'When I saw he loved hair, Your Majesty,' explained Daisy, 'I remembered Mr Mistry's parcel. It all made sense. One brush for each tentacle!'

The queen beamed. She was imagining the wonderful hairstyles an attendant with eight arms could give her.

Tom didn't look quite so happy. He nudged Daisy.

'Hey!' he whispered. 'Is your breathing bubble getting smaller? I'm *sure* mine is…'

Chapter Nine
A Gift from the Sea

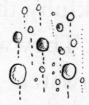

Tom was right. Their breathing bubbles were shrinking.

'It's getting harder to see through, as well!' said Daisy.

Tom's bubble, too, was becoming less transparent by the second. Soon neither he nor Daisy could see out at all.

Then suddenly both bubbles burst.

Tom and Daisy could see again. Thankfully, they could breathe, too. They were no longer underwater.

The children were back on Genie Street, outside Snippers.

'Thank goodness,' purred a familiar voice. 'A normal rear end!'

Jinx was there with them. He was looking lovingly at his tail.

'That was a *deeply* cool trip!' said Tom. 'But I wish we'd brought back a souvenir.'

Jinx cleared his throat. He casually held up a paw to display a huge, shiny pearl.

'After all,' he purred, 'it would be rather a shame if you forgot all about our little undersea adventure...'

Tom and Daisy beamed at him.

'Don't worry, Jinx!' said Daisy. 'We won't!'

Mr Bryant
SCARY
GIANT

Contents

Chapter One
Keeping Secrets

'Do we *have* to go straight home?' said Tom. He looked longingly at the magic street lamp. He and Daisy were walking back from Figbys' general store. They had been to fetch some milk for Mum.

'It's tempting, isn't it?' said Daisy. 'But we *can't*, Tom – not now!'

Daisy was right. Mum was waiting for them. They couldn't risk giving away the street lamp's secret – the secret of what happened when you rubbed it in a special way…

Once up,
Once down,
Then three times
Round and round.

They carried on walking. Moments later a ball of purple light shot past them.

The light-ball swerved left and hit the front door of number 12.

'But… but how did…?' Daisy stammered. She looked back at the magic street lamp. 'We didn't rub it!'

Tom had a good idea who *had* rubbed the lamp. There was a cat-flap in the door of number 12. Tom had just glimpsed the tip of a black and white tail disappearing through it.

Chapter Two
Out of the Blue

'That was Jinx, I'm certain!' said Tom. 'Going through the cat-flap in Mr Bryant's door!'

Mr Bryant was the nice old gentleman who lived at number 12. He was a retired train driver. He liked growing vegetables and woodcarving.

Tom and Daisy hurried to his front door.

'I didn't think Mr Bryant had a cat-flap,' said Daisy. She peered at the flap suspiciously. It was glowing purple. 'He hasn't got a cat, has he?'

Tom was about to shake his head when something bumped gently against the top of it. He looked up in surprise.

It was a sandbag. It was dangling from the basket of a large, stripy hot-air balloon floating just above them.

'Hullo, hullo! Look out below!' called a cheery voice.

A little man in a purple uniform was leaning over the side of the balloon basket. It was Mr Mistry, the Genie Street postman. He was holding out a parcel.

'Special Delivery!' he cried. 'By Air Mail, bless my ears!'

He let go of the parcel. Tom reached out and caught it.

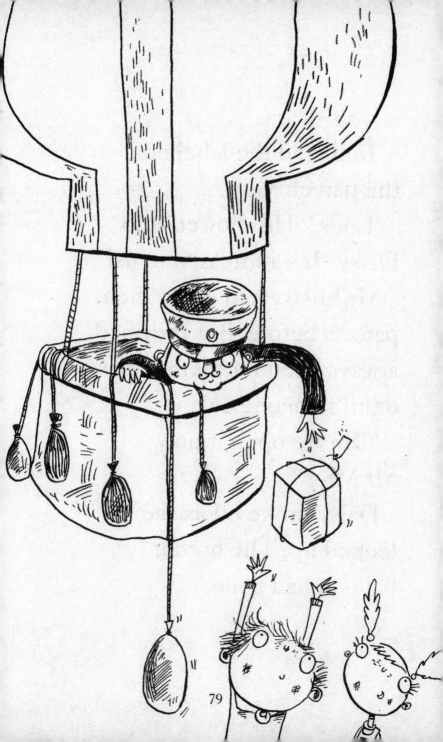

Tom read the label on
the parcel.

'Look!' He showed it to
Daisy. 'It's addressed to us!'

Mr Mistry had given them
parcels before. But they had
always been for them to pass
on to someone else.

'Can we open it now,
Mr Mi–?'

Daisy broke off as she
looked up. The hot-air
balloon had gone.

TOM
+
DAISY

81

Chapter Three
Through the Cat-flap

'Let's open it, anyway!'
said Tom.

Daisy nodded. She put
down the milk on Mr Bryant's
doorstep, and gave Tom a
hand unwrapping the parcel.

Inside, there were two
baseball caps. One had a 'T'
on it and the other had a 'D'.
Tom and Daisy tried them on.

'Woah! What's happening!' cried Daisy.

She and Tom were shrinking, very fast. Within seconds, they had become a tenth of their normal size.

'This is crazy!' yelled Tom. 'Look how *huge* everything is!'

The bottle of milk was now taller than they were.

Tom's eyes fell on the glowing cat-flap. *That* was bigger than them, too.

'Come on, Daisy!' said Tom. 'We must be meant to go through!'

Before his sister could reply, Tom had disappeared through the cat-flap.

There was nothing else for it. Daisy crossed her fingers. She dived through the flap after Tom – and found herself in the middle of a nightmare.

Chapter Four
Run for Your Life!

Someone was yelling.

'Run! Run! He's coming!'

There was thick green undergrowth all around Daisy and Tom. The voice had come from somewhere within it.

They heard a loud crash, and the ground shuddered. A few moments later it happened again. CRASH!

A little man in a leaf-green suit burst from the undergrowth. He had pointy ears.

'Didn't you hear me?' he yelled, as he dashed past Tom and Daisy. '*He's coming*! Run for your lives!'

There was an even louder crash, and the ground shook again. The children realized what the sounds were.

Footsteps. Very, very heavy footsteps coming closer.

Tom and Daisy sprinted after the little man. As they ran they tried to make sense of their surroundings.

They were in a forest. Its trees had the tallest, thickest trunks they had ever seen.

'Do… you… think…' panted Tom, 'we're… in… Lampland?'

'Uh-huh!' replied Daisy. She dodged some toadstools, then hurdled a massive pinecone. 'And… I think… we're still… tiny!'

The earth-shaking footsteps sounded closer and closer.

The children raced on, into a clearing between the massive tree trunks. Here, small wooden houses were clustered on the forest floor. It was a village.

'Oh, Tom!' gasped Daisy. 'How awful!'

Almost all the houses were wrecked. They looked like they had been crushed by some tremendous force. The village was deserted.

Up ahead, the little man had stopped running. He had found a hiding place. It was a dark hollow under a huge tree root. Tom and Daisy ducked into its shadow beside him.

'Keep *very* still and *very* quiet!' hissed the little man.

Tom and Daisy nodded. They tried to get their breath back as quietly as possible.

The heavy footsteps seemed to have stopped.

Chapter Five
Alf

The little man in the green suit was staring at Tom's ears.

'You're not elves?' he whispered to Tom.

Tom shook his head.

'No,' he hissed back. 'Is that what *you* are? An elf?'

'Of course!' The elf tipped his hat. 'Alfred Greenleaf at your service! Call me Alf!'

'Thanks for the warning back there,' said Daisy. 'What *was* that thing?'

Alf the elf looked grave.

'It is my people's greatest enemy!' he said. 'The terrible giant who stalks Elvenwood! It was *he* who trampled our village into ruins!' Alf's face darkened. 'And sometimes his *giant black panther* prowls the forest with him!'

Alf fell silent. The earth-shaking footsteps had started again.

One huge boot, and then another, crashed down only metres away from where Tom, Daisy and Alf were hiding. A shadow fell across them.

'Blast the wretched things!' boomed an angry voice. It rumbled above, like thunder. 'I'll find them if it's the last thing I do!'

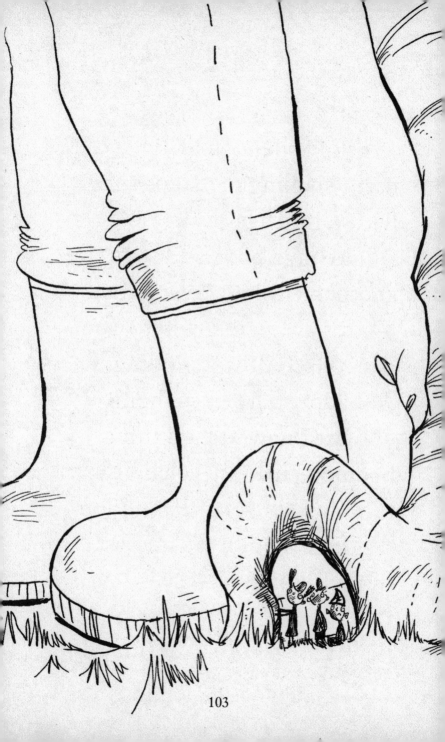

Chapter Six
Gotcha!

A gigantic hand reached
down to the forest floor.
Its thick, hairy fingers
began to grope around.

'I know they're here
somewhere…' rumbled the
giant's voice.

Tom, Daisy and Alf pressed
themselves back into the
hollow, trembling.

The giant's hand made
a sudden snatch.

'Gotcha!' he boomed.

He lifted his huge hand
close to his nose and peered
at what he had found.

He was clutching a
giant-sized pair of spectacles.
He had pulled them from a
tangle of undergrowth.

He put them on. A wide
smile broke across his face.

It was a face that both Daisy
and Tom recognized.

Chapter Seven
Things Become Clearer

The children burst from their hiding place.

'Mr Bryant!' cried Daisy. 'What are *you* doing here?'

The gigantic Mr Bryant looked startled.

'Blow me down!' he boomed, peering through his spectacles. 'Young Tom and Daisy! How did you get so *tiny*?'

'I've been trying to find my glasses,' continued Mr Bryant. 'I dropped them a few days ago!'

Daisy remembered that Mr Bryant always wore spectacles.

'It's been a struggle doing my job here in Lampland without them,' he went on. 'A forest warden who's as blind as a bat isn't much use! But now I can see clearly again!'

Things were becoming clearer to Tom and Daisy, too.

Mr Bryant *had* wrecked the elves' village, like Alf said, but without realizing it. He had trampled on it while stomping around the forest half-blind, without his spectacles.

When Daisy gently explained this to him, Mr Bryant was very upset.

'I'm *so* sorry, my dear little man!' he said to Alf. 'I had no idea! Please, tell me what I can do to put things right.'

Chapter Eight
A Big Help

Mr Bryant set about making up for the damage he had caused. Thanks to Tom and Daisy, he now knew about the tiny folk who shared the forest with him.

Alf and his fellow elves found that the 'terrible giant' wasn't so terrible after all. In fact, a *friendly* giant could be a big help.

Mr Bryant carved beautiful new houses for the elves. He even built a wonderful miniature playground for their children. The elf village was going to be better than ever.

Things were going very well until an unexpected visitor came calling.

'Run! Run for your lives!' yelled Alf – again. 'It's the GIANT BLACK PANTHER!'

But Tom and Daisy weren't at all worried.

The 'panther' was actually black *and white*, and *very* familiar.

'Hi, Jinx!' called Daisy.

The elves were amazed to see the children rush to greet the giant cat.

'Good afternoon,' purred Jinx. 'My, aren't we looking tiny today? Almost *mouse-*sized.' He gave them a wicked grin. 'Now, I think it's time we were on our way. So, if you'd like to hop on…'

119

Chapter Nine
Cat-flap Cavern

Tom and Daisy said their
goodbyes. They climbed up
on to Jinx's furry back. He set
off towards the part of the
forest where their adventure
had begun. They soon came
to the entrance of a dark cave.

'Cat-flap Cavern,' purred
Jinx. 'And our way home.'

He padded into the cave…

…and back out into daylight on Genie Street.

Tom and Daisy slid down from Jinx's back. Jinx knocked off their baseball caps with a casual flick of his paw.

Both children instantly grew back to their normal size.

'Oooo!' moaned Tom. 'That felt weird!'

Jinx looked up at them. 'Hmmmm… I think perhaps I preferred you *bite-sized*,' he teased.

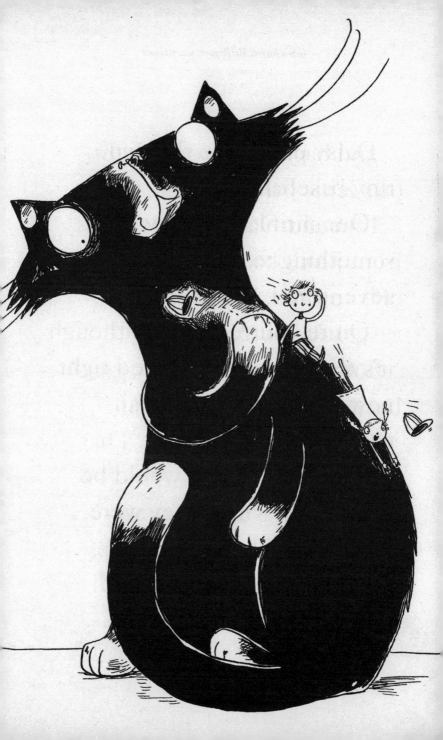

Daisy picked up the two tiny baseball caps.

'Our shrinking caps will be something to remember our adventure by!' she smiled.

'Quite,' purred Jinx. 'Although it's *thinking* caps you need right now – to come up with an excuse for your mother.'

It was true. Mum would be wondering where they were.

Daisy grabbed the milk. Then she and Tom headed across the street, for home.

GENIE STREET

Fan Pages

Here's what other children have to say about Genie Street and their favourite Lampland characters!

'My favourite part was when the octopus brushed Mrs Greene's hair.' Tilly, age 6

'I like all the characters but if I had to choose one it would be Daisy. She is so brave.' Poppy, age 5

'The story was good. There was a funny, talking cat and a crazy postman. I liked reading about the children visiting Lampland.'
Vincent, age 5

'I like the cat because he is cute!'
Emily, age 7

'I like the way they always have a souvenir at the end of the story to remind them of their adventures.'
Sophia, age 7

Parent note

Genie Street is a brand-new fiction series that
is the next step up from Ladybird's Read it yourself
Level 4. Ideal for newly independent Key Stage 1
readers, these books are for children who want
to read real fiction for the first time.

Collect all the titles in the series:

9781409312390

9781409312406

9781409312413

9781409312420

9781409312437

9781409312444

Each book contains two easy-to-read stories
that children will love. The stories include short
chapters, simple vocabulary and a clear layout
that will encourage and build confidence when reading.